This book belongs to

Karyn ♡

# *Barbie* in
# Unwelcome Guests

Illustrations by
Christian Musselman and Lily Glass

**EGMONT**

# EGMONT

*We bring stories to life*

First published in Great Britain 2009
by Egmont UK Limited
239 Kensington High Street, London W8 6SA

BARBIE and associated trademarks and trade dress are owned by,
and used under licence from, Mattel, Inc.
© 2009 Mattel, Inc.

ISBN 978 1 4052 4432 9

1 3 5 7 9 10 8 6 4 2

Printed in Germany

The Forest Stewardship Council (FSC) is an international, non-governmental organisation dedicated to promoting responsible
management of the world's forests. FSC operates a system of forest certification and product labelling that allows consumers to
identify wood and wood-based products from well managed forests.

For more information about Egmont's paper buying policy please visit www.egmont.co.uk/ethicalpublishing
For more information about the FSC please visit their website at www.fsc.uk.org

Hello, I'm Marina the mermaid and I live in the Coral Kingdom.

This is the story of what happened when our beautiful underwater home turned dark . . .

One morning, Marina woke on her cockleshell bed to find Coral Kingdom cloaked in darkness.

"Where is the daylight?" she wondered, swimming into the shadows. As she swam through the reef, trying to feel her way, she bumped straight into Curly, her little seahorse.

Curly seemed very upset. "Marina, the sea is so dark that all the fish are bumping into each other," he said, sadly.

"Let's find out what has happened," said Marina, blowing a long, bubbly note on her conch shell.

The little fish gathered round and peered through the gloom at Marina.

"I can hardly see my light," complained the poor lantern fish.

"I'm afraid of the dark!" wailed a tiny mitten crab, rubbing his eyes with a claw.

"My babies can't see their way," cried the angel fish. "Why is it so gloomy?"

Suddenly, a shoal of angry fish swam through the darkness towards Marina.

"Calm down!" said Marina. "Whatever's the matter?"

"Come and see," the coral fish grumbled, leading Marina and Curly to their beautiful coral garden.

The coral was covered in hundreds of shiny creatures with long, sticky suckers and big, blinking eyes.

As Marina swam nearer to the creatures, they squirted jets of black ink from their tails.

"They're spoiling our coral home! They're making it dirty!" cried the coral fish, waving their fins angrily.

"Shh," Marina hushed the fish. Then she looked kindly at the creatures. "I'm Marina and this is Curly, my little seahorse. Who are you?" she asked.

"We're squinklets," squeaked one little creature, "and we would never spoil the reef on purpose."

"It's true," said a little voice. "It's not the squinklets' fault at all."

"Who said that?" Marina asked, looking around.

A little sea-girl swam out from behind a pillar of coral.

"I did. I'm Azura, the Coral Gardener," said the little girl. "I look after the coral gardens of the ocean and the squinklets help me."

"But why did they use their ink to make Coral Kingdom dirty?" Curly wondered with a frown.

"We squirt ink to keep ourselves safe," peeped one tiny squinklet, "and to protect the reef, too."

"Bad things are coming," said Azura sadly. "The Gatherers are on their way. They glide through the ocean with their webs, scooping up the prettiest fish and munching the coral."

"We try to hide the coral from them," sighed the squinklets, "but they always find it."

That night, as the sea creatures slept, a big, dark shadow floated towards the silent beach.

With two long, spiky legs, it began to spin a huge, strong web that hung beneath the surface of the water. Another shadow joined it, and another, and they spun their own webs. Soon, there was an army.

The Gatherers dived to the bottom of the sea. Silently, they trawled the seabed on eight long legs, scooping up the prettiest fish and chomping on the coral they found in their path.

Azura awoke, and saw the Gatherers not far away, their webs bulging with fish.

The fish were darting to and fro, trying to escape. The stingray tried to sting its way out and the razorfish tried to cut at the web with its razor, but it was much too strong for them.

"Don't worry," whispered Azura. "I'll fetch help."

Azura shook Marina's shoulder to wake her. "The Gatherers have found us!" Azura cried, and the two of them swam to the coral garden to ask the squinklets for help.

Marina told the squinklets what to do, and with worried eyes, they swam after the Gatherers.

The squinklets stuck their extra-strong suckers to the webs and tugged as hard as they could. One by one, the webs came loose from the Gatherers' clutches, setting the fish free! The fish darted swiftly in front of the Gatherers, confusing them and making them dizzy.

The squinklets squirted more ink and soon the Gatherers could not see at all. With an angry groan, the Gatherers gave up and swam away with empty webs and empty bellies.

Marina swished her arm through the inky water.

"Oh dear," she laughed, "I think our beautiful home could do with a spring-clean. The corals and sponges are very dirty and inky."

"Can we help?" chorused the cleaner fish, Spick and Span. "Cleaning is what we do best!"

"We can all help," said Marina. Soon Coral Kingdom rippled with activity as the sea creatures began to scrub and polish.

With every wave, the water grew a little clearer.

In the clear light, the friends saw what had become of the coral garden. Pieces of coral lay on the seabed, bitten off and crushed by the Gatherers.

"Oh dear," sighed Marina. "Our beautiful garden!"

Then Azura swam forward. "I have something for you," she said shyly, holding out a pouch woven from reeds. "It's coral dust," she told Marina. "There isn't much, as it's very rare, but you can use what we have. It will help your coral garden grow again."

Together, Azura and Marina sprinkled coral dust over what remained of the garden.

The squinklets clung to the coral and squeaked.

"We're sorry we said you'd spoiled our home," said the coral fish, blushing. "Please stay!"

"Will you stay, too, Azura, and be our coral gardener?" Marina asked the little sea-girl.

Azura smiled sadly. "I must look after all the ocean's coral gardens. I will come back and visit, though."

As Marina waved goodbye to Azura, the sun rose, and the beautiful, clear waters of Coral Kingdom glistened once more.

Magical titles available in this series:

Look out for more enchanting tales to add to your collection!

# My *Barbie* Story Library

Barbie Story Library is THE definitive collection of stories
about Barbie and her friends. Start your collection NOW
and look out for even more titles to follow later!

ISBN: 978 1 4052 3105 3 • RRP: £2.99    ISBN: 978 1 4052 3106 0 • RRP: £2.99    ISBN: 978 1 4052 3107 7 • RRP: £2.99    ISBN: 978 1 4052 3108 4 • RRP: £2.99    ISBN: 978 1 4052 3109 1 • RRP: £2.99

# A fantastic offer
# for Barbie fans!

In every Barbie Story Library book like
this one, you will find a special token.
Collect 5 tokens and we will send you
a brilliant double-sided growing-up
chart/poster for your wall!

Simply tape a £1 coin and a 50p coin
in the spaces provided and fill out
the form overleaf.

**STICK
£1 COIN
HERE**

**STICK
50p COIN
HERE**

NOTE: Style of height chart
may differ from that shown.

cut along the dotted line and return this whole page

To apply for this great offer, ask an adult to complete the details below and send this whole page with a £1 coin, a 50p coin and 5 tokens, to:
BARBIE OFFERS, PO BOX 715, HORSHAM RH12 5WG

☐ Please send me a Barbie™ growing-up chart/poster. I enclose 5 tokens plus £1.50 (price includes P&P).

Fan's name: .......................... Date of birth: ..........................

Address: ..........................

..........................

Postcode: ..........................

Email of parent / guardian: ..........................

Name of parent / guardian: ..........................

Signature of parent / guardian: ..........................

Please allow 28 days for delivery. Offer is only available while stocks last. We reserve the right to change the terms of this offer at any time and we offer a 14 day money back guarantee. This does not affect your statutory rights. Offers apply to UK only.

☐ We may occasionally wish to send you information about other Egmont children's books, including the next titles in the Barbie Story Library series. If you would rather we didn't, please tick this box.

**Ref: BRB 001**

cut along the dotted line and return this whole page